D0186271

This book
belongs to:

- - - - - - - - - - - - -

WITHDRAWN

Essex County Council

3013021140572 4

For Jenny Hayes, with thanks and love,
K.S.

Sir Charlie Stinky Socks would like to donate 10% of the royalties
from the sale of this book to Naomi House Children's Hospice.

EGMONT
We bring stories to life

First published in Great Britain in 2016
by Egmont UK Limited
The Yellow Building, 1 Nicholas Road, London W11 4AN
www.egmont.co.uk

Text and illustrations copyright © Kristina Stephenson 2016

Kristina Stephenson has asserted her moral rights.

ISBN (HB) 978 14052 68134
ISBN (PB) 978 14052 68141

A CIP catalogue record for this book is available from the British Library.

All rights reserved. No part of this publication may be reproduced, stored in a retrieval
system, or transmitted, in any form or by any means, electronic, mechanical, photocopying,
recording or otherwise, without the prior permission of the publisher and copyright owner.

Stay safe online. Egmont is not responsible for content hosted by third parties.

THE MUMMY'S GOLD

Kristina Stephenson

EGMONT

Once upon the drifting dunes

of a **desert** in a far-away land,

three figures were dutifully trudging

over the shifting sand.

A **burly baker**,
who used to be a **pirate**,
had sent them on a quest:

to return a bag, stolen from
someone in a **desert**
across the sea.

"I've given back the rest of our booty.
Now all that's left is this," he said.
"It's **bashed** and **battered**
and **terribly tattered**,
but it might be precious to that *someone*.

The thing is . . .

I'm too busy baking
to return it."

And that's how it came to be that . . .

...Sir Charlie Stinky Socks,
his faithful cat Envelope and, of course,
his good grey mare, were there, in the **desert**
with a bag and some buns on the
brink of a brilliant adventure.

For inside the bag was:

a stick,

some string,

a stone that looked like a *toe*, and . . .

a little leather journal.

How to Find
The
Mummy's
Gold
by
Elfie CoRRie
Age 6
Please return if found

What could be hard about that?

But, gosh! It was hot!

And not a good place to discover
your bottle's been leaking.

Yikes!

Poor parched cat and overheated horse!

What *were* they going to do?

Just then a **caravan of curious camels** came cruising into view.

"Salutations!" said Sir Charlie
to the *fellow* at the front.
Might we trouble you for a drink?
I don't think my friends and I will make it,
if we haven't any water."

"Make it to where?" asked the *friendly fellow*.

"We're looking for someone," Sir Charlie replied.
"Someone called **Elfie Corrie**.
I believe this bag belongs to her,
because it says so on this book.

Look!"

The *friendly fellow's* eyes lit up.

"**Elfie Corrie!**" he said.
"I know where she lives.
And there's a watering hole
on the way.

Why don't I take you there?"

The knight and his cat were glad of the ride.
The good grey mare wasn't sure.
But it wasn't long before they came to an oasis.

"Drink your fill," said the *friendly fellow*.
"I will make camp for the night."

He lit a fire, pitched his tent, and told Sir Charlie and his friends to go in.

"Sleep," he said. "I'll keep watch. I don't want your bag to be stolen."

ZZZZZZZZZZZZZZZZZzz

It was already hot when the friends woke up
to find the **camels** had **gone** –
along with the *friendly fellow.*

Sir Charlie scratched his head.

"Well, at least we still have the bag," he said.
"And this tent will come in handy."

It did!

In the guise of a **camel** the good grey mare sailed across the **desert**.

Swish, swish, swishity-swish!

Straight to a one horse town and . . .

CORRIE'S CURIOSITIES
MUSEUM OF MARVELLOUS THINGS

OPEN

Noticing the name was the same as **Elfie's**, Sir Charlie ventured in . . .

ME!"

"Gadzooks!" said
Sir Charlie Stinky Socks –
he wasn't expecting *that*.

Or the story the old lady told him
over a cup of tea.

A trove of treasures
filled the room and
behind the counter was a little old lady
with hair as white as snow.

"Good morrow," said Sir Charlie politely.
"I've come to return this bag.
Pirates stole it from **Elfie Corrie** –
a little girl you might know."

"Know **Elfie Corrie**?" the lady replied.
"Why, **Elfie Corrie** is . . .

"You see, when I was six," **Elfie** said, "I planned a **really big adventure**.

I'd heard the stories about the missing **gold** of the **Pharaoh Aboo Ra** – lost in the desert for thousands of years.

So I decided to find it!

I wrote down clues in my journal
and collected things to use on the way,
until inside my bag I had **everything** I needed
to find the **mummy's gold**.

Except . . ." she said,

"for one last thing and
while I was searching for it,
someone stole my bag."

Oh my!

"When I grew up," Elfie continued, "I became an explorer.
I found all kinds of trinkets and treasures,
but I didn't find my bag.
So I never had my **really big adventure** and now . . .
I'm just too old.

"That's silly!" said Sir Charlie kindly.
**"You're never too old
for adventure**.
And I'd be happy to help you."

Elfie thought for a moment or two.

Then she smiled at the little knight.

"By golly, you're right," she said
to Sir Charlie. "**Let's go and
find that gold.**"

She opened her bag
to take out her journal, but . . .

"I saw those feet on the
way," said Sir Charlie.
"And my . . . erm . . .
camel can take us there."

Clue number 1:
Two giant feet
stand alone in the sand.

"Not to worry," said **Elfie**. "He's got the journal, but he won't
find the **gold** without the other things in this bag.
I might be old," she said with a smile,
"but I've still got the clues in my head."

. . . where *was* the little book?

Oh no!

"That **not-so-friendly fellow** I met
must have taken it," said Sir Charlie.
"I'll bet he's after the **gold**!"

Trudge, trudge, trudge, trudge!

Over the shifting sand, to the remains
of a statue with only nine toes.

"**Clue number 2!**" said Elfie.

"**When the last toe lies
in its rightful place,
behold the secret door.**"

Elfie took out her toe-shaped stone.

But that's when
Sir Charlie saw the *not-so-friendly fellow*!
He'd got to the feet first.

Drat!

Time for a mare with a bag of buns to tempt the **camels** away.
Off they trotted after the buns, followed by the
not-so-friendly fellow who wanted his **camels** back.

Elfie popped the toe
in its place and . . .

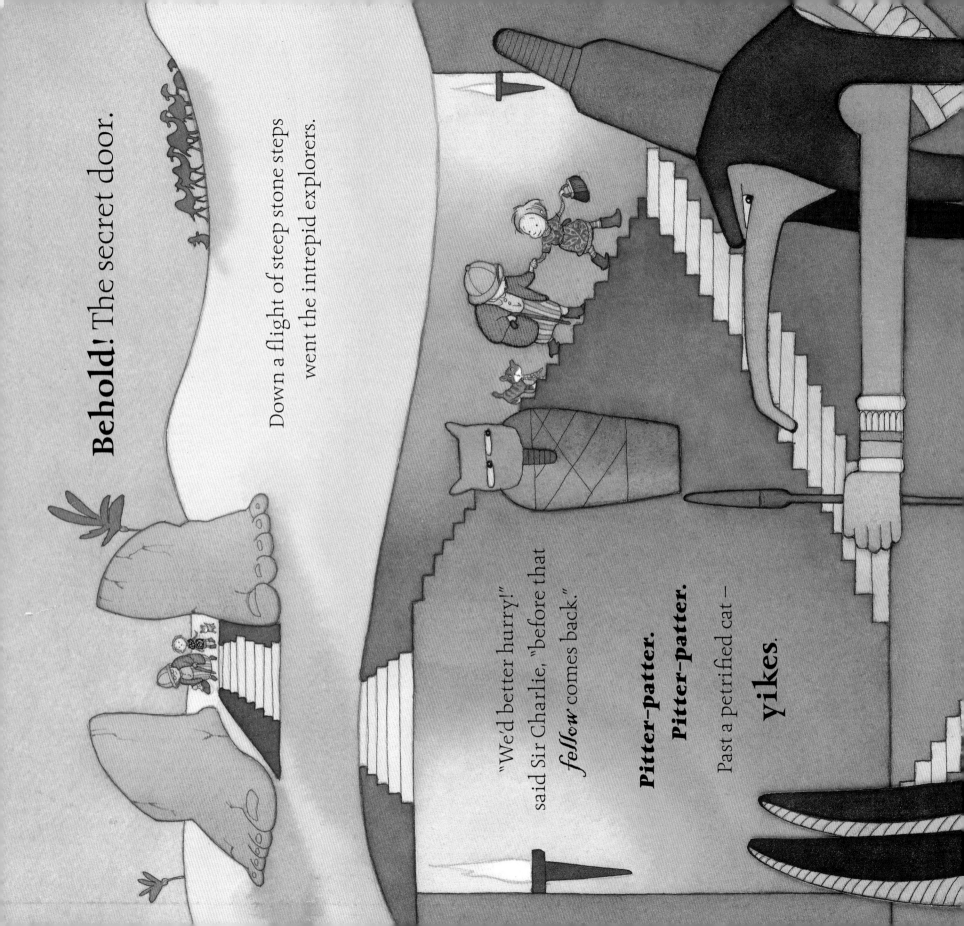

Behold! The secret door.

Down a flight of steep stone steps went the intrepid explorers.

"We'd better hurry!" said Sir Charlie, "before that *fellow* comes back."

Pitter-patter.
Pitter-patter.

Past a petrified cat —

yikes.

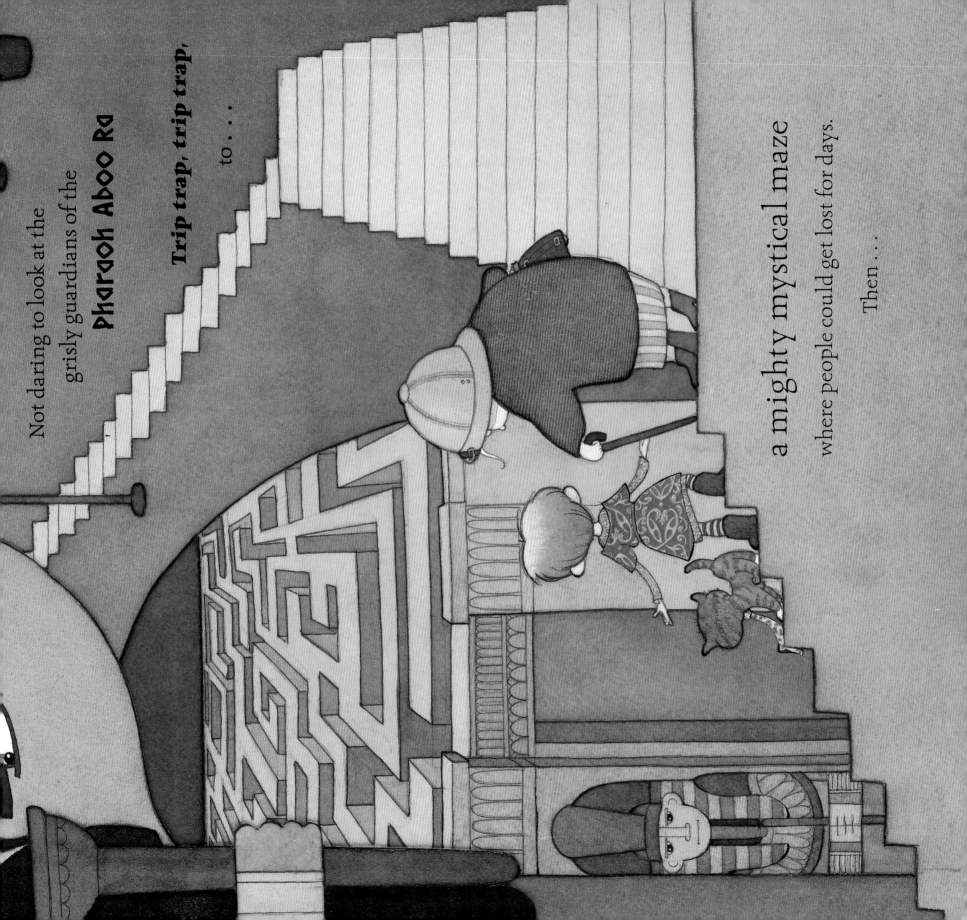

Not daring to look at the
grisly guardians of the
Pharaoh Aboo Ra

Trip trap, trip trap.

to . . . .

a mighty mystical maze
where people could get lost for days.

Then . . . .

Elfie remembered the next clue.

**"String will bring you back to safety,
should the path you take be untrue."**

"Got it!" said the clever knight, fastening one
end of **Elfie's** string to a figure on the wall.

"One wrong turn," he said to the others,
"and we simply follow this back.
Anyway . . . I'm good at mazes."

Maybe you are too?

Start

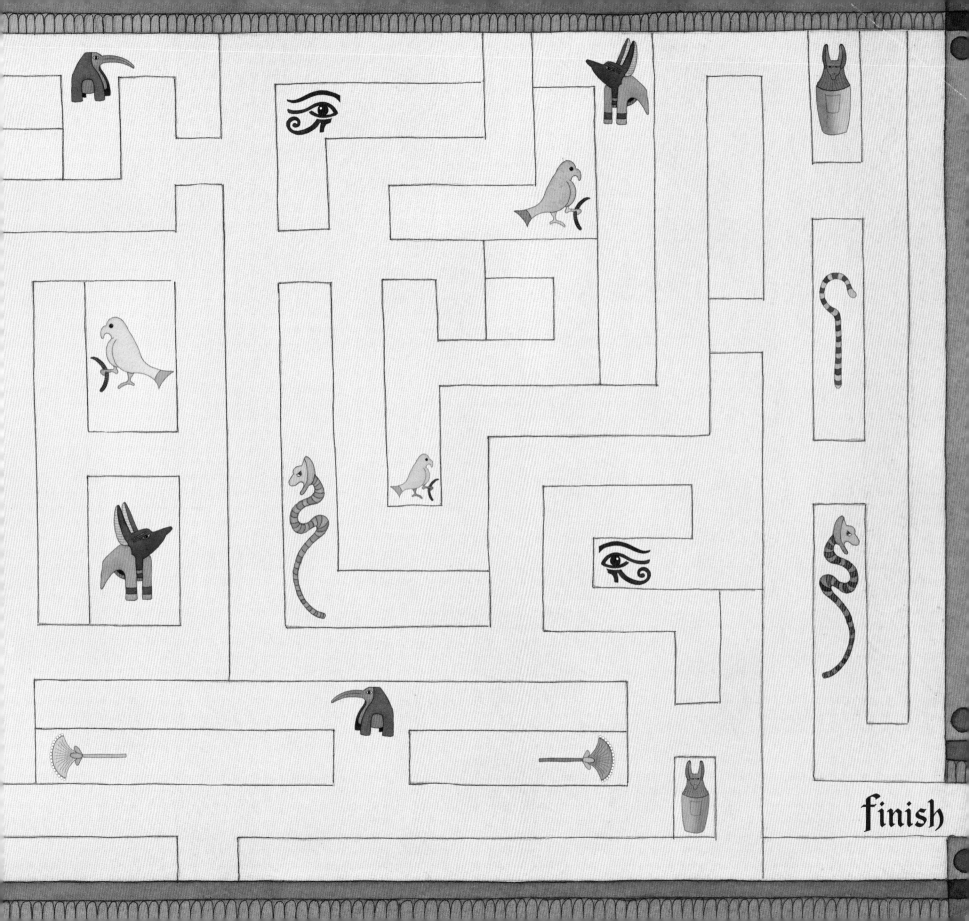

finish

Beyond the maze was a decorated door.

It was locked.

There was no way in.

"Botheration!" said Sir Charlie.

But **Elfie Corrie** was smiling.

"Look at the picture
on the wall," she said.
"It's just as I thought
it would be.

Elfie smiled at Sir Charlie Stinky Socks.
The little knight had been right –
you're never too old for adventure

and . . .

there just might be time
for one more.

THE END?

"I'm sorry," he said when he saw **Elfie**, and he handed her the book. "I only took it because I wanted to have a **really big adventure.**"

"Then we'd better make sure you have one," said **Elfie**. "Come to my shop tomorrow. I've got **marvellous maps** from around the world; one of them should do."

Oh what luck!

They were just in time.

Back came the *not-so-friendly fellow*, leading a line of munching **camels**, and a mightily proud, grey mare.

Glittering **gold** and untold *treasures*
filled the ancient tomb,
and in the middle stood . . .

the **mumbling mummy**
of the
Pharaoh Aboo Ra!

"Thieves!"
he grumbled, "you've come
to steal my **gold**."

The key to opening this
tomb is my stick –
the staff of **Aboo Ra**.
But it can't be done
by just anyone;
it HAS to be . . .

a cat.

That's the thing
I was trying to find,
the day my bag was stolen."

Envelope's moment had come.

The **mummy** heaved the saddest sigh.

"I knew this day would come," he said,
"and I don't think I can bear it."

"But I don't want your **gold**,"
said Sir Charlie.

"And all *I* wanted," said **Elfie**, "was a really big adventure. So stop your worrying, my dear. I'll leave this stick with you, and we'll bury the little stone toe. Without them no-one will find your tomb, and your treasure will **always** be safe."

"Zounds!" said Sir Charlie. "What about the journal? The *not-so-friendly fellow* might come back and the secret door is still open."

Quick!

Out of the tomb.

Back through the maze.

Up the steep, stone steps.

Through the feet.

Shut the door.

Hide the little stone toe.

"Jeepers creepers!" thought the quaking cat as the **mummy** shuffled towards them, **mumbling, grumbling** and **fumbling** with his bandages.

Then . . .